M

This Is the GAME

By Diane Z. Shore
& Jessica Alexander

Illustrated by
Owen Smith

HARPER
An Imprint of HarperCollinsPublishers

This Is the Game

Text © 2011 by Diane Z. Shore & Jessica Alexander

Illustrations © 2011 by Owen Smith

Manufactured in China.

Library of Congress Cataloging-in-Publication Data

Shore, Diane ZuHone.

This is the game / by Diane Z. Shore & Jessica Alexander ; illustrated by Owen Smith. —
1st ed.

  p. cm.

  ISBN 978-0-06-055522-1 (trade bdg.)

  ISBN 978-0-06-055523-8 (lib. bdg.)

  1. Baseball—Juvenile poetry. 2. Children's poetry, American. I. Alexander, Jessica.
II. Smith, Owen, date, ill. III. Title.

PS3619.H665T54 2011   2008047700

811'.6—dc22   CIP

                                                                          AC

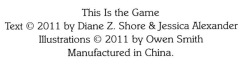

Typography by Jeanne L. Hogle

11 12 13 14 15   SCP 10 9 8 7 6 5 4 3 2 1

❖

First Edition

To Dad, a die-hard Cubs fan, who taught me the rules
of the game

—D.Z.S.

For Grandma, who gave me long drives, Texas skies,
pudgy pies, and all the things that make a summer
special . . . and in memory of Grandpa, who loved a
great game

—J.A.

For August and Walden

—O.S.

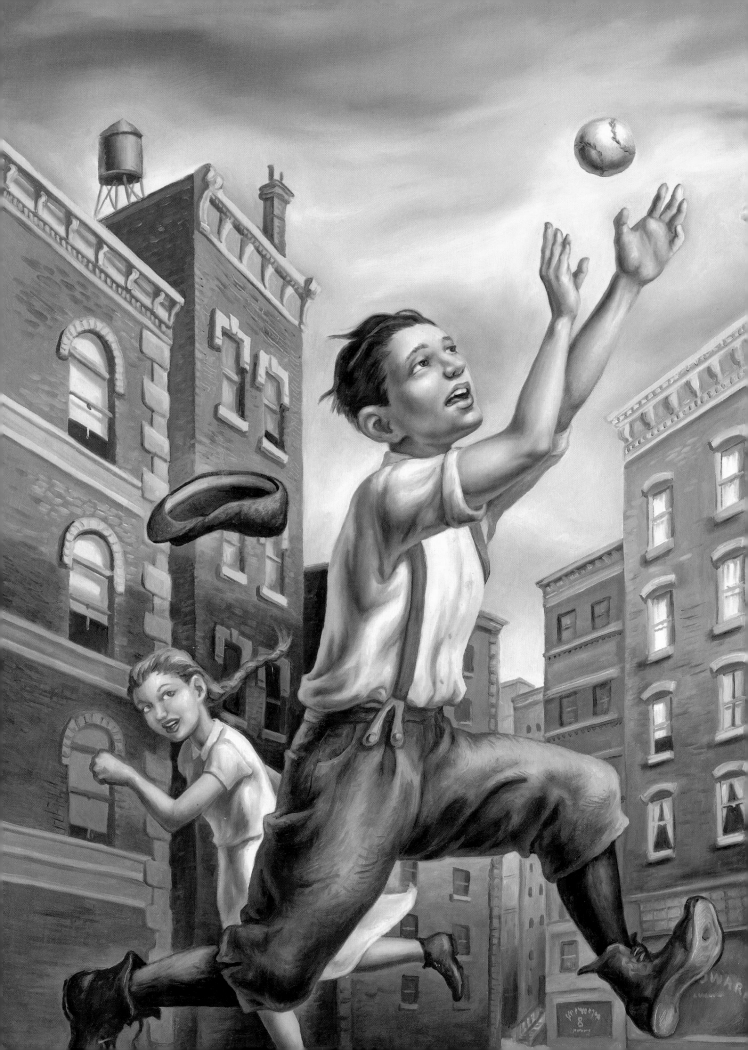

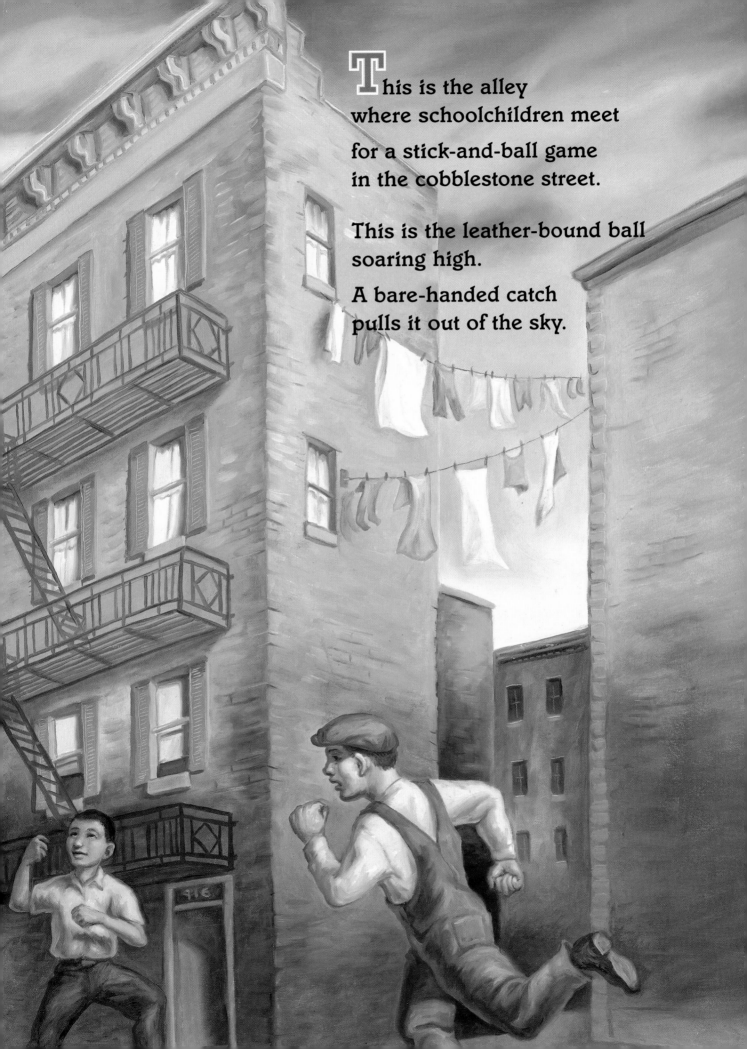

This is the alley
where schoolchildren meet
for a stick-and-ball game
in the cobblestone street.

This is the leather-bound ball
soaring high.
A bare-handed catch
pulls it out of the sky.

This is the bat, a bottlenecked club
the batter keeps perfectly sanded and rubbed.

These are the players, rounding the bases.
Winners score twenty-one runs known as "aces."

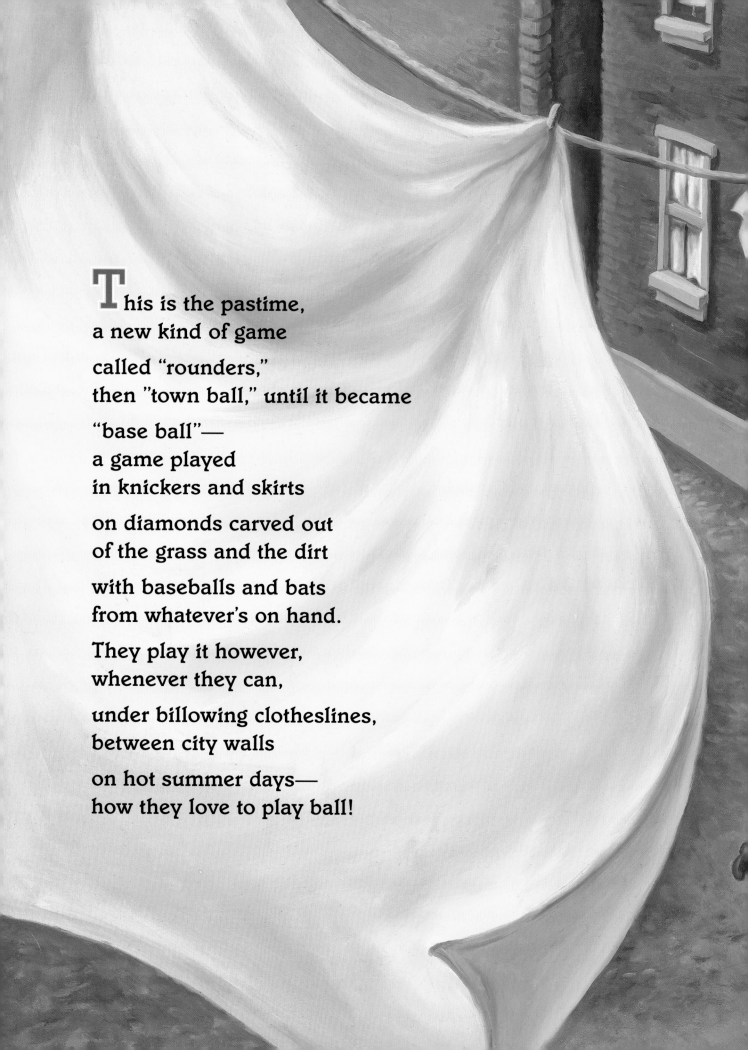

This is the pastime,
a new kind of game

called "rounders,"
then "town ball," until it became

"base ball"—
a game played
in knickers and skirts

on diamonds carved out
of the grass and the dirt

with baseballs and bats
from whatever's on hand.

They play it however,
whenever they can,

under billowing clotheslines,
between city walls

on hot summer days—
how they love to play ball!

This is the grandstand with tall wooden bleachers
where fifty cents pays for a nine-inning feature.

This is the pitcher they call "Dizzy" Dean.
Hold the bat steady—his fastball is mean!

This is "the Babe," "the Sultan of Swat," clearing the fence after calling the shot.

These are the major leagues: uniformed teams offering heroes with World Series dreams.

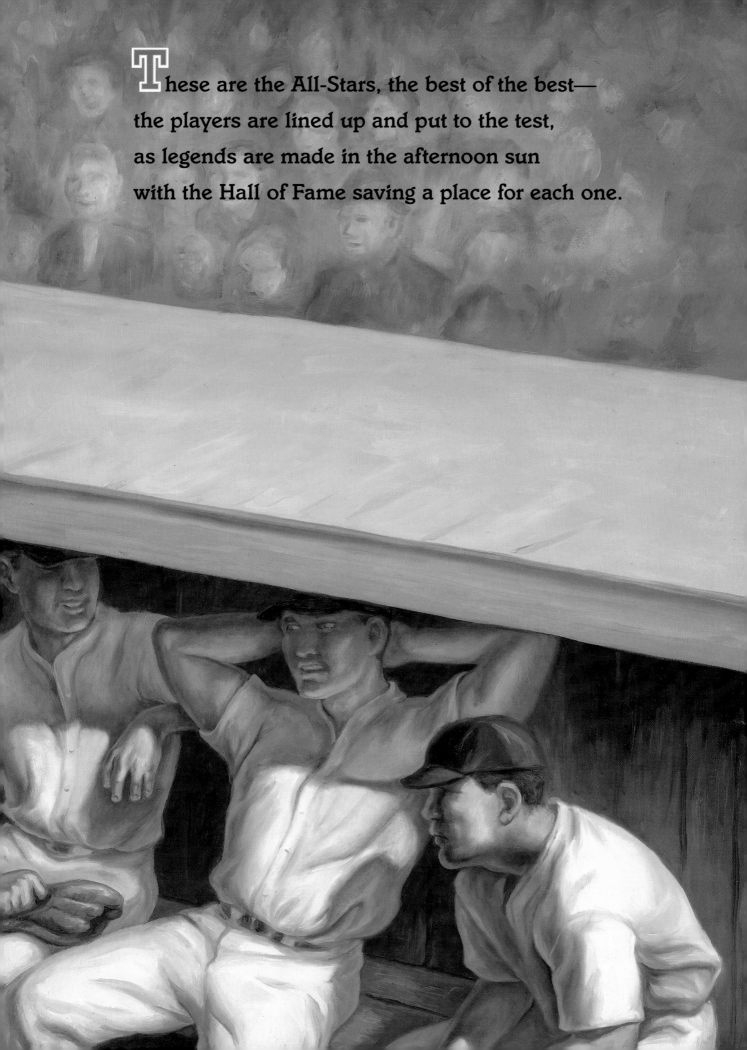

These are the All-Stars, the best of the best—
the players are lined up and put to the test,
as legends are made in the afternoon sun
with the Hall of Fame saving a place for each one.

And tucked inside pockets on bubble-gum cards
are the men kids become when they play in their yards,
while under the scoreboard, they root for them all,
wave banners and sing as their heroes play ball.

This is the ballpark flooded with light,
bringing the afternoon game into night.

This is the windup, and this is the pitch:
spin, curve, or wobble—the catcher knows which.

This is the hit: "Going up . . . and away!"
The radio broadcasts the full play-by-play.

This is the Dodger
fulfilling a dream,

a Negro Leagues star
joins a Major League team.

This is the season
and this is the inning—

a Major League change,
a historic beginning

when young Jackie Robinson
wears Dodger blue

and helps to make
one single league out of two—

while a crackling radio
broadcasts the sounds,

and on the front porch,
neighbors gather around

marking their scorecards,
awaiting the call,

as all kinds of people, together,
play ball.

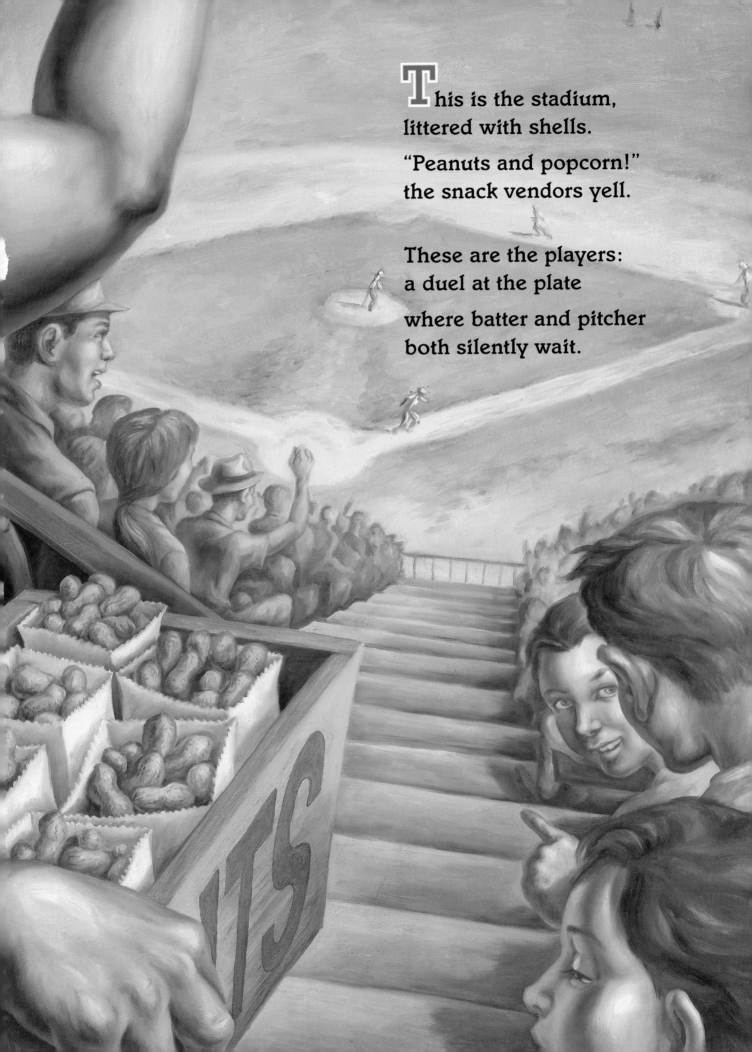

This is the stadium,
littered with shells.

"Peanuts and popcorn!"
the snack vendors yell.

These are the players:
a duel at the plate

where batter and pitcher
both silently wait.

This is the *swish!* as the pitch whizzes by
from the mound to the plate in the blink of an eye.

This is the *crack!* as the bat meets the ball
and sends it careening out toward the back wall.

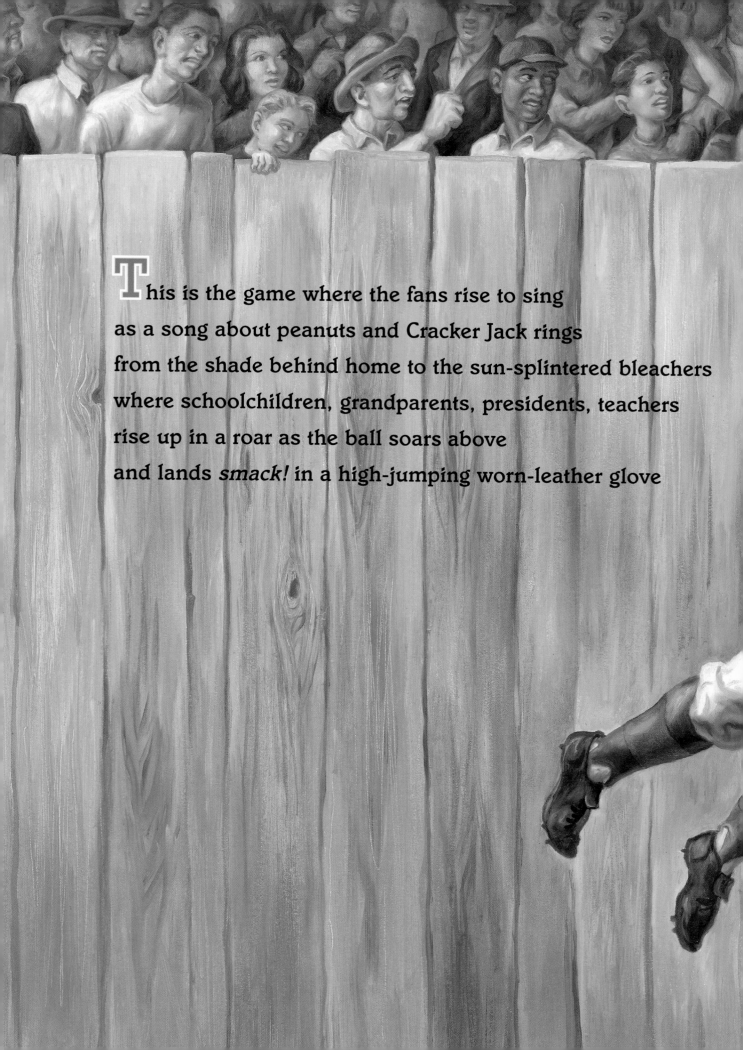

This is the game where the fans rise to sing
as a song about peanuts and Cracker Jack rings
from the shade behind home to the sun-splintered bleachers
where schoolchildren, grandparents, presidents, teachers
rise up in a roar as the ball soars above
and lands *smack!* in a high-jumping worn-leather glove

for the game-saving catch: then, exploding in cheers,
the home team piles up, the rest "wait till next year"
in the spring, when we'll once again come to the park
for the sights and the sounds and the rhythm and spark
of this ages-old pastime that captures us all

and begins when the umpire bellows,

"Play ball!"